The Little Book of Modern Fables for Adults (45 Original Fables on Life, Love and Work)

Volume I

By Edward Johnson

INDEX

The Kingwalk

Few of us are born with one destiny, one dream, one all-encompassing purpose. But that is how it felt for Leo. Leo's job was to prevail over the prey, the pride and the plains. Like a general, he ruled over life and death for lions and everything else.

Surprisingly, Leo was a 41-year old accountant from Bournemouth.

Not really, he was a lion. And for miles around, he was the lion. When pretenders to his throne growled in protest, he bared his teeth, flicked his mane, and let them hear his roar. He then watched them leave at impressive speed.

What more could he want?

Well actually, he wasn't satisfied. And this had been going on for a while. As you might expect, he decided to get into skateboarding. And this helped. Until one day? Disaster.

Leo came off and got whacked in the mouth. Badly. He got fixed up, but it wasn't the same. He wasn't the same. Baring his teeth and roaring was what he did. He decided to leave. He had never felt lower, and he struggled with each day.

Somehow he ended up outside an ice cream shop.

"You want an ice cream, kitty?" said the owner.

"Kitty?! What's an ice cream?"

"Well there is frozen milk and sugar and..."

"I'll have one."

The ice cream was easy to eat with his still bruised mouth, and tasty too. Leo started to frequent the ice cream parlour more and more. But soon, his money began to dwindle. He told the owner of his problems.

"Would you consider a job with my brother?" Leo agreed to meet him.

As is sometimes the case, the ice cream shop owner's brother was a leading fashion designer. "Oh, look at the hair? Look at the legs? Those shoulders? Someone fan me, darling! I can't cope with this! This... majesty!" And Leo smiled. He was offered a job there and then.

Within a fortnight, Leo was doing catwalks in London, Milan and Paris. He also did Pontarddulais, which was a bit quieter. He loved it. The whole magic and over the top nature of it, plus some whacky and wonderful clothes.

"Leo owns the catwalk!" said the papers.

"It's not a catwalk, it's a kingwalk!" his fans shouted.

"Big cat is less catty than some models!" said a gossip magazine, but that wasn't the important point. The important point was that Leo was happier than he had ever been.

Sometimes the beach lies beyond the brambles.

2

Eye Nose Ewe

Yaldana-Kepler and Rymantica were two young female Gludarklings on the planet Sproog. Both featured in high society and frequented balls and gala events. They talked of their peers and parties. And no party was more fabulous and famous than the Trirhinovine Ball.

Even though it was months away, the girls talked of little else. What they'd wear, what they'd eat, and who they'd dance with.

Although the girls were great friends, they were also great rivals. They would try to outdo each other in their appearance. At one event, Rymantica had the entire guest list's names temporarily tattooed on her back in precious metal. But even that had been outdone by Yaldana-Kepler, who had the guest list projecting from her eyeballs all night. At the Frog Party, Rymantica had her tongue enlarged for the night, and whipped it at people's ears. Yaldana-Kepler had the same operation, but she'd also had her eyes enlarged and her pores exuded an intoxicant that made it a night to never forget.

Rymantica and Yaldana-Kepler were both committed and creative, but Yaldana-Kepler was also ridiculously rich.

But it was Rymantica's spies who found out what Yaldana-Kepler was planning this time. Perhaps Rymantica could finally get the limelight? Alas, when she discovered Yaldana-Kepler's plans, she knew she simply couldn't compete. For Yaldana-Kepler was having her skin greyed, her back furred, and a third eye! The cost of a third eye made Rymantica's head spin! And it wasn't just for the night. This would be for the entire season! Rymantica longed to have that sort of money. She'd have a third eye then! And a fourth! Maybe a second nose too! But she wasn't rich like that.

Desolate, Rymantica told her dressmaker to "do as he wished." The night came, and she put on the contextually simple dress. She was so miserable that she would have loved to have said she hated the dress, but the design, line and fabric were elegant. She might not be the main attraction, but she might even have a passable night.

She was warming to the occasion when Yaldana-Kepler walked in as if she owned the place (which she did).

"Oh my goodness!" almost shrieked one. Others drew their breath! But even before Rymantica saw her, she knew the gasps were in shock of Yaldana-Kepler, not awe. For she looked distinctly odd.

"She's gone too far this time!"

"The frog thing was a triumph, darling. This is a failure, darling. But don't tell her I said that, darling?"

It was not long until the crowd looked for their belle of the ball.

"What a simple dress, but absolutely beautiful! And no gimmicks! So brave, so kookichoo!"

"Kookichoo indeed, darling!"

Rymantica realised they were looking at her. And as she looked for her friend to comfort her, she was glad she didn't have the money for a third eyeball.

Be thankful for your blessings in disguise.

3

The Circle

One day an angel came down and got the attention of humanity (which wasn't too difficult, what with being an angel and all). The angel said they needed to communicate with everyone. The world busied with television, the internet, and radio. For remote places, extreme measures were put in place. And the angel spoke in such a language that all would understand.

The countdown to the angel addressing the Earth was the most exciting time anyone had ever known. Suddenly there were just seconds left. And then, with a special kind of light around and of the angel, they appeared on the screen, with running commentaries on the radio for pockets of the planet which could not be reached any other way.

The angel said hello and smiled.

Everyone smiled back.

Then the angel got a pen out and went to a board. The angel drew a circle. A perfect circle. And then the angel left the stage.

There was a hushed silence, awaiting the angel's return. But the seconds turned into minutes.

"The angel is not coming back!" some said. Broadcasters said that humanity would have to work out the meaning of the circle. Observers said the meaning was clear, although it was not so clear that they agreed upon it. Three main conclusions abounded, as the planet grew frenzied with discussion within moments.

"The circle is the sign of time. History repeats itself. We must learn not to repeat the mistakes of the past. Life is not a straight line. We must improve ourselves to deal with the challenges ahead, whilst never forgetting where we have come from."

But others thought differently.

"The circle is the Earth. We are to embrace it and love it and love each other. When we realise that, life is easier. Do we all not benefit from the multitude of riches of another's land, from the wonders of other's cultures? We prosper and learn from our neighbours, and them from us! We are all Earthlings first, members of lesser factions second!"

There was a third idea that also found favour.

"It is impossible to draw a perfect circle freehand for one of us, but we must aspire to perfection. This is about becoming the best each of us can be, and that will unlock the potential of ourselves and of the planet. Is that not clear? When one has the perfect circle, it serves as the perfect target to focus on for the future!"

As the people began to argue, the angel reappeared on the stage and screen, smiling. There was a global hush.

"I'm terribly sorry, my pen ran out. I had to find another one, and it took me ages! Oh, and I like your ideas, this talk is going to be easier than I thought for some of you!"

The simplest of things may teach us wisdom if we are open to learning.

4

The Dimeback

Rosemary was a sweet young girl with foghorn voice and a plucky spirit. She was always small for her age, and for that reason some thought of her as cute.

One person who did not think that was Violet Shackenbloomer. She was a powerhouse in Rosemary's school, teaching baking and American football.

"You're too short, and you're not strong enough, Rosemary." Amazingly, this was what Violet Shackenbloomer told Rosemary in cookery class! "You won't reach the table! It's too heavy for you!"

"Well I can't help being small! And I'm growing!" piped up Rosemary, who was rarely quiet.

"No you're not," said Violet. And sometimes it seemed that was the case, for Rosemary towered above nobody in the school, even when she was one of the older girls.

Now if Rosemary didn't care for cooking or American football, the story might end here. But Rosemary's walls were a mass of baking and American football posters. She lived and breathed both.

"You are too little to mix the bowl, Rosemary! Your cakes are rubbish! And there has never been a successful American football player your size! You'd be rubbish, you would! You have no chance!" She seemed to enjoy tormenting the young girl. And it was true that Rosemary's American football career's highlights were three uneventful minutes off the bench.

When Rosemary came to leave school, it was with her tongue poking out at Violet Shackenbloomer.

Leaving school seemed to make Rosemary flourish in so many ways, many of which she could have never imagined. But Rosemary's ambition had been fixed long ago.

And she practiced. And she learnt. And when there was a problem, she researched another way. And when there wasn't another way, she invented another way. She thought of new ways.

And she kept playing American football. She played for the worst team in the worst league. But slowly, she gained some trust and confidence of her teammates. "I want to be quarterback," she said.

"But you're so little, and…"

Rosemary cut them down with her foghorn voice. "This isn't a height competition! It is about getting a ball across the line!" And she detailed the way she would use her height, her voice, and how their team would be much improved from it.

They agreed to try it once. After that, only journalists asked about her height. And after her second Superbowl victory, she was yet again interviewed on television. Rosemary had been told that her old American football teacher would be on the programme. Violet Shackenbloomer tried to smile and hug Rosemary, but she held back. "Are you pleased to see your old teacher, Rosemary?" asked the reporter.

"Well let's put it this way: here's a pie for you, Violet."

Violet Shackenbloomer pursed her lips with glee. "And what type of pie is it, dear?"

"Humble. Now I suggest you eat every bit of it!"

Many things are impossible until someone does them.

5

Mr. A Bit Above Average

Everyone said Jonesy had a twinkle in his eye. When they met, Mrs. Jones said it was because he had fallen in love with her. Their kids said it was because he was fun, had secret plans and a mischievous sense of humour. And his friends and work colleagues said it was because he was always up to something.

And they were all right.

Jonesy worked in a fairly good job for fairly okay pay. He could have gone further, but he didn't want to. He played sports, and he enjoyed them. Again, he could have done more, but he was happy. They had a home that was lovely and happy without being grand. And they did things and ventured here and there. He treated his wife, but they watched the budget together as well. They were extremely lucky, albeit they had largely made their own luck.

Jonesy retired after his wife, and his children had taken their academic and training success into the workplace. He saw them find partners that made them happy, and soon his mischievous sense of humour was being put to good effect with the grandchildren. In his earlier years, he had been supportive and enabling of his children, but the fruits they enjoyed were unquestionably borne of their own labour. However, in his later years, he became occasionally lavish.

When he died, it was a sorry blow. But there was no doubt he died a rich man.

The family knew that his spending in his later years had surely diminished his estate. That was no concern, because he had made sure Mrs. Jones had no financial worries long before, and the children were in good jobs, and knew how to handle money. It was something of a shock when they found that Jonesy was a multi-millionaire. Indeed, his wealth was well into eight figures. The solicitor's office was filled with a mix of shock and elation. Plus, a little uneasiness over him keeping such a secret.

After the hubbub had died down, the solicitor read a letter from Jonesy which talked about his family and his love for them, and then turned to the money.

"I have been an extremely wealthy man many years before I met my beloved wife. But the wife I yearned for would be attracted by love and vision, not bling and baubles. I trusted her completely, but I knew that two people would struggle with such a wonderful secret, and I was concerned my children would have their futures plagued by such riches. The value of the money and their efforts would be diminished if they looked upon themselves as heirs to a fortune. I felt this would have been a distraction from their natural progression in life, and that at a certain level, money was likely to hinder them more than help them.

I know that this news will come as a shock, and I know you will not meet it with full agreement or jubilation at the start. Yes, you could have had tickets to every big game, taken your friends in a private jet, and impressed with a Ferrari. Or even two. But I hoped that by taking this different course that your mother and I would see you grow into exactly the people you have done. And now that you are settled, is at least a part of you not glad that you got the money after meeting your partner? I know that you might also think that the money could have been used for good. Trust me, it has. And that includes charities and local issues, which I have noted in a journal provided with my will.

In any event, it will take a little time (probably more, knowing solicitors!) for the final settlement to be with you. During this period, I suggest you keep this secret from your partners and your children. If you decide to tell them, you don't have to tell them the correct amount. I hope you enjoy this money, but I would invite you to consider following (and no doubt improving on) my methods. Because for all those riches, the lives you have lived and the people you have become are far more valuable. I love you all."

Later that day, the children told their partners of an emotional get together and of their father's will. No, the money wasn't massive, but they expected that. One explained in detail what she would get. "You liar! You are clearly lying!" said her husband. Her heart skipped a beat. "You've got his twinkle too!" And he wasn't joking.

And Mrs. Jones smiled over a cup of tea. He was gone, but his happy mischief lived on.

Enough is as good as a feast.

6

Conduction, Convection and Radiation

Ava and Val sat in Ava's kitchen chatting nonsense with gusto. When their conversation turned to their love lives, their mood darkened.

"Salvatore is a nice guy, a great guy. And I could really go for him. But it just doesn't seem to be going anywhere." Ava let out a wistful sigh.

"Well you've only been together eight months," said Val.

"Nine," corrected Ava. "Anyway, what about you and Dmitri?"

"Well… I mean, you already know. He was really keen, I wasn't. Then we sort of broke up. Then I asked him back out, but he'd gone a bit cold on the idea. And then, well you know it all anyway."

"And now?"

"I don't know." She half laughed.

"Ask Sammy, I always ask Sammy."

"Yeah, Sammy our guru!" They laughed. And resolved to ask Sammy.

*

"What you've got to remember, and this goes for both of you, is the sun and the land and the sea," said Sammy.

"Okay, is this going to be deep or involve science and geography?" Val joked.

"Maybe all of them. Okay, now just because two people like each other and it would genuinely work between each other, it doesn't mean they arrive at the same place in the same way at the same time."

"Well that makes sense, Salvatore is always late!"

"What I'm saying is this. Just say the sun is love?" They smiled and cooed and laughed. "We'll look at Val and Dmitri, because they've been together, on and off, for a bit longer. The sun is love, and Dmitri is the land. And you, Val, are the sea. It takes a type like Val longer to warm up, but when she does, that heat stays. Whereas Dmitri was affected by the heat of the sun faster, but it cooled faster too."

"So we're never going to feel the same at the same time?"

Sammy laughed. "Listen, I'm no expert. But the land and sea don't just accept the energy from the sun. The land and the sea react with each other. Sea breezes, land breezes, and so on. It's a cycle."

"So I have to wait? How long Sammy, I want a precise date!" Val smiled.

"Six weeks, three days and two hours! I don't know! If I knew, I wouldn't be single!"

People warm and cool to ideas at their own pace, and patience and understanding concerning this may bring rich rewards in all areas of life.

7

I spy, something beginning with "e"

The judge got up and was five minutes behind schedule within her first cup of tea. She'd grab something at lunch. Anything. But then she saw her husband had left her a packed lunch on the side. Healthy, no doubt. The diet would not be slipping today it seemed.

Her day was spent with a case of theft. There was some little issue over identification, but the prosecution energetically covered that. Then there was also a small point on motive, but they keenly dealt with that too. So she found the defendant guilty.

After work, she was meant to run with her friend. She was meant to phone her, but if she waited then she might get out of it. But her friend rang her.

"What about if we run five miles instead of three?"

And the judge was caught unawares and couldn't think of a reason not to.

Five miles and a shower later, and she collapsed with a cup of tea. The phone rang. It was her sister asking if she could pop around. And she wasn't keen, but was too tired to think how she could say no.

The judge considered her extremely strange day. Because often it would have been easier to acquit the thief, to skip training, or to run less, and to put off her sister. And as for her diet? Well, that was more off than on. A big part of making things happen is people not finding easy excuses not to.

People habitually look for the easy way out.

8

A hippo's skin is about a quarter of their weight

Some dates were good, and some were bad. This was in the middle. She knew she didn't really fancy him fairly quickly. It was just that something wasn't there. But they'd had a nice night. And because she kind of knew him (a close friend of a friend, and they'd spoken lots), they had ended up popping in to her house for a cuppa. Plus, he had said he really needed something to drink quite badly.

The cuppa was finished, the conversation slowing, and he'd be gone shortly.

So she thought.

The clock ticked onwards and he still showed no sign of going. She said how she had better go to sleep soon. He said he should get some sleep too, he was very tired.

The conversation was at a stop. She had to sleep. He said he was too tired to drive. He would sleep in his car, but it was cold and uncomfortable. Perhaps the couch? And ten minutes later, she was asleep in her bed as he took the couch.

She didn't get up that early, so thought he may well be gone. But when she went downstairs, he was watching her television with a coffee. He said hello, and asked what they were up to that day. Struggling to wake up, let alone deal with this, she said she had lots of things to do. Very busy. Very. In fact, she had better get to it. She imagined that he had things to do too. He agreed that he did. She thought that would hurry him up.

But when she came downstairs from her shower to say she had to go, he was still not ready. She said she didn't mean to rush him, and he said that was okay. And then dragged his feet to an unbelievable degree. He said he could let himself out. It wasn't that she didn't trust him, but this was where she lived and he did not. He said he had urgent things to do, and so she decided just to leave rather than carry on with this farce.

An hour and a half should do it, she thought. But when she returned he was still there. "Not to worry," he said, "I've managed to put off what I had to do. What are we doing for lunch?" She winced.

But maybe lunch would get him out?

He drove them to lunch. Finally, he was out of her house. At the end of lunch, he gave a shocked face. "I've been on the vodka oranges, I forgot I was driving!" Her jaw dropped. "I'll get us a taxi to yours." She didn't know what to say. He explained how his friend would drop him to his car later.

His friend was on his way. And then he wasn't. And then he'd ring back. And then it was night. She offered to take him, but he said he couldn't have her do that. At worst they'd do it in the morning. He asked what her plans for the weekend were? Suddenly, she saw just how practised he was, and how he saw his leaving as a ball he would bat back to her until she tired. And then she snapped and told him to leave. She'd drive him to his car immediately. And when he said it was a bit late anyway, she said he had better get out of her house now or else!

"No need to be like that, don't know why you're being funny with me!"

He had been on time for their date, but he had been a day late leaving.

Never underestimate how thick some people's skin can be.

9

In search of Hubert's skill

Everyone loved football at Hubert's school. But Hubert wasn't very good. Some were less into it. Some played rugby, a few boxed or did martial arts. Hubert wasn't good at them. They had other sports: cricket, gymnastics, baseball, hockey, swimming and athletics. He wasn't too good at those either. Which was fine. After all school is more about the academic side.

Hubert wasn't great at the academic side. But then there were the extra-curricular activities. The clubs; chess, fishing, amateur dramatics, music, etc. He was universally mediocre (at best!) at everything he tried.

But being a kid is also about having fun. Games, exploring, computer stuff.

Nope, you guessed it.

But Hubert did have determination. He resolved to find his skill as he reached adulthood. Art (drawing, painting, sculpture), trading on the stock market, working with animals, climbing mountains, anything and everything! He kept a book of what he had tried and what the result was. He was not an out and out failure in everything, but he was a sure fire thing at way under par (except in golf, where he was always way over par).

As his search got more extreme, the things to try became less. He'd tick off archery, knitting and orienteering one week, and record each defeat in his book. But at least there was one thing less to try.

Of course, sticking at something was the key to almost everything. But even when he tried that, it didn't work either.

He began trying more and more unusual things in a search for his true skill. But when you aren't cool enough for Morris dancing, or marrow growing competitions, you may have a tough job on your hands.

Hubert sighed as he boarded the train (don't ask about Hubert's driving!). Today was a shed building course. He'd read up on it, he actually quite liked the sound of it, and he was rather hopeful. He switched off his mind a little (which was overdue) and fell asleep. Rather predictably, he woke up realising he was past his stop and very late. And then he saw his book.

A woman was reading it. She was seated next to him. He had left it on the empty seat, and she had picked it up.

Then he realised why he had woken up. She was laughing. At every misery and disaster which he had endured and faithfully recorded in arduous detail.

In fact, she couldn't stop laughing.

He seemed to wobble between wanting to cry and laughing himself, and somehow he came down on the latter side. Just.

"Why this is marvellous! I haven't read anything so brilliant, so funny, and so original in years! In years! Did you write this?"

He admitted that he did.

"Why you must have the most inventive mind I have ever known! How did you make all these things up?"

He blushed a little. "I didn't. They are all true." This made her laugh harder. Much harder. Tears coursed down her cheeks. The rest of the train carriage were a mix of embarrassed and entertained.

Finally, she regained control of herself. "I'm sorry, I'm sorry. Look, I'm a publisher." She reached in a case and held out a card, which he took. "Please tell me you don't have a publisher already?" He shook his head. There was a look of excitement on her face now. "My office is just by the next stop, and I would very much like to publish your book, Hubert" (it said "Hubert's Book" inside the front cover).

He smiled like never before in his life, but then his smile dropped. "I am meant to go on a shed building course today though."

"If you come with me, you can buy any shed you want. You're a brilliant writer, and you are about to make a lot of money!"

Hubert beamed. "Okay then! Although I won't need to buy a shed, I live in a flat."

And she began laughing again.

Everyone has a special talent. It just takes some a little longer to find it.

The World of Dog Eats Dog

The boardroom was a rich affair of burnished wood and shiny metals, with windows overlooking the city.

The company's top brass filed in, greeting each other with handshakes and slaps on the back. Their coffees were brought to them, and the time for their training with the trainer was minutes away. They didn't know him, but they did know he was meant to be a hotshot. There was a collective nervousness as the colleagues all pondered how to impress him (and potentially stab a work rival in the back, should the opportunity arise).

9 am. The door opened and he smiled. After the briefest of introductions, he walked to get some water. He got their attention and slowly poured the water into the glass. "Okay, who can tell me how this represents the here and now of this company?" He spoke slowly and confidently.

They all had answers, but only a few were brave enough to get the ball rolling. The trainer liked the answers, but he warned they were just a first step. "After all, why should you be here today? As in what should we try and get out of this meeting? Because we've got the people in this room to change this company for the better right here and now! Today!"

He made eye contact with them, and let that statement hang heavy in the air. The responses were coming faster now. He had one of them note them down on a board.

One suggested they should discuss the detail of the recent figures that had been posted. The trainer said that it was a good point (one of several good points and good questions), and one to get onto after strategy for today's purposes.

Then he said he wanted them to write notes to each other, saying what they felt they could do to help the other person, what the other person could do to help them, and what they might do together to help others and the company. "No point is too small! Nothing is criticism! We are trying to make a difference here, and your considerable talents can get this company better for everyone, including yourself and each other!"

Even though the room held several rivals, there was a momentum within the room and they felt compelled to comply with this awkward task.

Finally, the trainer told them a true story that had shaped his life. And the audience sat in rapt attention.

After a most unusual morning, they broke for lunch. As the session finished, the managing director entered the room and shook hands with the trainer.

The MD turned to the room, "A good morning, troops? I hope the training went well?"

"Excellent!" "Really helpful!" "He really knows his stuff!"

The MD sighed and got out his chequebook. Then he wrote a cheque to the trainer. "Okay, you can tell them now."

The trainer turned to the room. "I am not a trainer. I don't actually know what your business is. Your boss hires my fishing boat. I made him a bet that I could come in here with no information and have his managers thinking I was an expert sent to teach them. He said you were much too smart." He smiled again as he picked up the cheque.

And the room went very quiet.

You can't please most of the people most of the time, but you can certainly fool a lot of them some of the time.

11

Rocket Man

Robbie didn't consider himself a normal man. Because he was twelve feet tall, could easily lift a car and was made from metal. Yes, Robbie was a robot.

He was shaped like a man though, and his manner and mind had been based on humans. So he was arguably more like a man than anything else.

And he was certainly more like a man than anything else on Mars. Lonely Mars, uninhabited and nearly uninhabitable. Just Robbie to do his work day after day. Take the readings, send them to Earth. Build the base, mix the fuel, charge himself back up overnight.

Ah, mixing the fuel. Rocket fuel. Sweet rocket fuel.

For reasons involving radioactive interference, Robbie's charging base was five kilometres away from the landing base where he worked every day. For months he trekked back every night.

Then one night, instead of turning to his charging base, Robbie went to towards the rocket fuel. After all, he could run off several different types of energy. Moments later, the coarse liquid was entering his system. His joints shook as his system struggled with the acrid mix. It wasn't the best way for him to recharge, but he could take it. And it was just this once.

News of the incident reached Earth. The scientists discussed it, saying something must have gone wrong. For some reason, Robbie had to take these extreme measures, and it was surely a one off.

Until the found out he was doing it every day. Messages were sent to Robbie for him to stop using the rocket fuel. There were cost implications, his body would deteriorate and his mission would be compromised.

Robbie listened. That night he went to his charging base. And the next. But then he didn't for a week. He said he would the next day, but then he didn't.

Message after message came from Earth, and he began to ignore them. His logic circuits knew they were right, but something in him had been compromised it seemed.

Then he got an unexpected instruction from Earth. It told him to travel half a kilometre towards his charging base. This seemed utterly pointless, but it was an instruction so he resolved to follow it. The first steps were the most alien; he had not walked that route for several weeks now. But one of the scientists had worked out that there was a magnetism attracting Robbie from all the machinery and equipment at the landing base. That made taking the first steps much harder. But if he got five hundred metres away, the pull of the landing base would be weaker at every step.

The scientists watched from Earth. It took Robbie as long to do the first half a kilometre as for him to do the remaining four and a half kilometres. A cheer went up.

The concern was the next day. Again, Robbie was told to walk the first five hundred metres on his own. It worked. After a week, they stopped telling him. They monitored him, but he seemed to be good as new, back to his old routine. And life on Mars began to settle down, with its beautiful orange skies, an average of minus 80C, and lethal dust storms.

With bad habits and addiction, small steps today are better than the promise of big step tomorrow.

12

She Could Lose Three Gloves

"Yes, so wear gloves, don't wear a scarf, and don't wear jeans so tight you can't move on the ice."

Why did he bother? She stood before him with a scarf that could have been made for a giraffe, jeans that looked painted on, and said, "I forgot my gloves, shall I have yours?"

Last year was mad enough. An hour of constantly trying to keep her upright on the skating rink as she came out with the classic, "I'm going to get my phone out and take a photo as we skate!"

She declared she was having a drink before she went on. "A wine would be very nice!"

"Do you think drinking is a good idea? Especially when you can't skate anyway?"

She looked forlorn. "But you taught me last year, remember?"

"I'm not sure pulling you around for an hour a year ago means you can skate." She smiled, deciding to only hear the last three words as she headed towards the bar.

They approached the front of the queue to get their skates. "Oh, I think I've lost one of your gloves, sorry! Didn't I lose them last year as well?"

Her first scrabbling steps onto the ice shocked her. For she was sure she could skate, and yet she was clearly unsteady. "Something wrong with the ice here," she concluded.

"Yes, I think they are using different ice now."

"Are they?"

"No."

"Oh! Well I think we should take selfies before we skate off. I'm okay to skate on my own, before you ask again."

"Then I'll skate off. I think we did enough selfies in the car and the queue." And with that, he set off and breathed a sigh of relief. He was not the best skater himself, and set off a little cautiously.

Three photographs later, she bounded forwards, and then downwards. Maybe trying to take the photograph at the same time was too much to do immediately. She fell again. More power, that's what she needed. He helped her up. "Maybe I should help you around until you get into it a bit more?" She took his hand.

After the first circuit, she decided to try a twist! The beginning was the trick, she reckoned.

They fell in a heap, him groaning. He limped off the ice, as she decided to go on a little longer. Until the stewards saw her fall again, and said maybe she should rest. What did they know? So she'd fallen down twelve times! And maybe caught a few people. This was skating. They weren't the ice police! But after the next crash, she admitted defeat, and the pair found themselves walking around the fair. Moments later, he had been overruled as to them going up in a carnival ride with carriages that whizzed around, high in the air.

He knew it was a bad sign when she covered her ears during the safety message. And whereas he breathed hard, she made a joke of trying to move her safety bar on her lap.

Perhaps in frustration, or to distract himself from the height they were reaching, he thought of her constant aberrations. There was the boss she threatened with the High Court, her insistence she wouldn't have put petrol in her diesel car, and her telling the stables she was an experienced rider. He was away in his thoughts, thoughts of her never listening.

Out of the corner of his eye, he spied her teetering dangerously out of the seat with her arm outstretched to take yet another photo. He called to her, but if the rocking of the carriage wasn't stopping her, why would his voice? He strained to try and reach her.

The ride began to turn, and she sat back down hurriedly. Then she jumped up again, "Maybe one more!" she cried with her phone in her hand, gleefully tormenting him over his fear for her. But she didn't get to sit down again, because ride had spun into life, and her words and life were lost in the whip of the air as she careered downwards.

You can't help some people.

13

The Long Brass Neck

There was once a giraffe who fell upon hard times. In the summer, there was a lot of film work. But in the winter? And the cost of scarves was always a problem. Plus, the leaves had fallen from the trees. The giraffe was tired and hungry.

"Come with us," said the hyenas to the giraffe. And they went along and together chased some poor animal down. The hyenas feasted until they had had their fill, and the giraffe went to eat. But the hyenas had taken every morsel of flesh from the body.

"Are you having a laugh?" said the giraffe. It seemed they were. The giraffe wandered off disconsolately.

Then he came across a rhino.

"Looking very raffish there!" said the rhino.

"I've been mixing with the hyenas."

"Oh no! Oh you don't want to do that, dear boy! You must have been desperate!"

"I was! I'm so tired and hungry, and I'm broke!"

The rhino grinned. "Why come work for me? I work part-time charging people until they break, and part-time as a lawyer. There isn't much variety, really."

So the giraffe worked for the rhino. But it turned out that the rhino was a very crooked lawyer, and even tried to extort money from clients and others when it was not due. The giraffe made no money from the venture, and animals called out abuse to him. The rhino mocked him when he quit. "You've got to have a thick skin in this business!"

Exhausted by his efforts, the giraffe walked across the plains. He came to a withered tree, on which perched a vulture. Again, the giraffe relayed his tale of woe.

"You could have it easy! Just use that long neck to fetch the money from the bottom of that well! Plus, you can have a drink!"

"There won't be water in that well! Look how dried up the tree is? And why would there be money in the well?" inquired the giraffe.

"The well is deep, there's water there alright! And people throw a coin in the well and make a wish. If I could reach down like you, I'd have been rich long ago!"

"Isn't it stealing their money though?" asked the giraffe.

"Maybe."

"And it looks a very dirty well!"

"Well, have a bubble bath after then!"

So the giraffe stuck its long neck down the well. And it was only when its head hit the bottom that it realised just how filthy it was. And there was no water and not a single coin. And that was exactly the moment when the vulture started taking pecks out of the giraffe's ass. But it was the vulture's cackle that stung even more as the giraffe walked away, filthy, hurt and upset.

You can always stoop and pick up nothing.

14

The Errant Son and the Foolish Father

There once was a rich man with a son who did not succeed. He did not work hard in school, in jobs the father got for him, or in the father's own business. Time and again, the father tired of his son's lack of effort. But he would relent, and make things as easy as could for the son to try again on each occasion. He would buy him a car to travel, pay off his debts so he could focus on whatever the son said he was doing next, and champion his cause when others doubted how it would turn out.

Finally, the father decided that enough was enough. He told his son that he could not simply walk away from another job or venture for some spurious reason. He said he would not support his son anymore. His son protested that he would not, and the father was emotional at the future he now saw for his son.

Weeks passed, and the son was again unemployed of his own making. He went to his father and beseeched him for another handout. At first the father refused, but he soon relented. He believed his son had learnt a lesson and was due to turn his life around. The pair left with both smiling.

Months passed, and the situation would come to repeat itself again and again. The father invited an old friend to his large house. The old friend knew father and son well, and the father told him of his woes.

"I wanted him to become qualified, skilled, a success. I have supported him in that."

The old friend had a look of sympathy, but stern words. "Your son is qualified and skilled in getting money from you. You have become his job. It is an easier one than the 9-5, and he need merely charm the coins from your hand when the need arises. And every time he cons his father, the old fool warmly embraces his son for doing so. It is a job he has worked hard at over the years, in contrast with every other type of employment he has tried. He has no intention of leaving that employment."

The father mulled over the words and went to reject them. "Ah, but I will not be here forever, and my son is intelligent enough to know that. And then where will he be?"

The old friend smiled. "The son's current position also has a pension that comes with this rather fine house, for he does not intend to work forever."

Wanting to help another may be driven by the heart, but make sure it is controlled by the head.

The Karate Fighter

There are several styles of karate, and a multitude of governing bodies (with their own touches of Machiavellianism). But the style he trained in had "kumite" (or fighting/ sparring) involving light contact. So a person would kick and punch to the face and body, but with such control as to not leave a mark.

The local champion had held a course the year before. He had gone. He was a black belt himself, albeit not a fighter like the champion. At the end, everyone had sparred with each other. The champion picked people off with punches and kicks with ease, but for whatever reason seemed to struggle with him. "Stop" was called to the sparring, and he turned away to go and bow. At that point, the champion had stood down on the back of his leg and then hit him from behind so that his ears were ringing. Within minutes, the training session was over and nothing came of the incident. He was shocked by the cowardice and sadism, especially from a champion and for no real reason, but there was little he could do.

He concluded he could not go to a competition or the champion's club and remonstrate or fight. He would just train, and wait for his moment.

And now the champion was again visiting to hold a course, this time in his very training hall (or "dojo"). The first parts of the session passed unremarkably. Then the students began to spar. He did not overtly seem to seek to spar with the champion, but he placed himself near to him. The champion's malevolently amused grin showed he remembered him, when he was not sure that he would. There was no look of concern though; after all, he was the champion.

The champion dodged and feinted, trying to draw an attack as he often did. But the man had waited for the champion to come to him, and he would wait until he came right into his little circle. For the man was not as fast as the champion in many ways, but he could rule that small circle that surrounded him. And so he waited, as they moved around each other. The champion grew increasingly frustrated, and the man wondered whether he would launch an attack before time was called.

But then he did. And he shifted to the side and blocked and countered at the same time. His punch sending the champion's head back, his face already contorting in pain. Not seriously hurt, but the swelling and bruising would be a painful reminder to him over the coming weeks.

Sometimes the answer is to focus on the small circle that surrounds you.

16

The Dirty Man

There was a man arrested by the Police for fairly minor offences. He had many previous convictions. When he was in custody, he defecated around his cell.

A young Officer looked in particular abhorrence and asked if the man had mental health issues. The senior Officer replied that he did not.

"But why would he do such a thing?"

The senior Officer thought deeply. "I cannot say, for people are different. And if you had seen his home, you would know he certainly does not enjoy being in filth. Neither is he so virulently anti-Police that it would explain this. But his repeated crimes have driven everyone from him. His partner, his family, his friends. The Probation Service have told judges they cannot work with him. He is not a success out of crime, and not a success in it. Or anywhere else. And he knows that. And every person wants to think they make an impact, have some power to make an impact on their world."

The young Officer took the words in. "So he resorts to the power to shock?"

The senior Officer smiled. "No, not to shock. He often does this, so it comes as no surprise. The only power he has is to disgust. But I'm not sure possibly knowing why helps us."

Even apparently deranged acts may possibly be understood, but that does not make them smell any sweeter.

17

The Two Karateka

Two girls started karate at around the same time. Both enjoyed it greatly, and progressed through the years to their black belt. They competed with comparable success.

The first began to arrive a little early, so as to warm up more. She would stay late and go through her techniques. At home, she would practice again and again.

The other was just as enthusiastic, but whilst her friend took every opportunity in the class to train harder, she preferred to relax and chat. She reasoned that if they had been more or less equal for several years, that little would change at this stage. For some time, she seemed to have been proved correct.

There came a day when both found themselves against each other in the final of a large competition. They battled with punches and kicks, and the fight was close fought. However, it was the first girl that convincingly won.

Their sensei congratulated them both. The second girl spoke to the sensei, and remarked that there was hardly anything between their speed and technique. Her friend's extra training was not the reason for her success, in her opinion. That another day, she felt she would have been the victor.

"Ah," said the sensei, "that may be the case. But I do not think so. Karate, and other arts and much of sport, comes down to angles and inches. And whilst doing that extra bit of training may only make a very small difference in one way, it may be a decisive small difference."

Much of sport is decided on angles and inches. Working hard for a small improvement may make all the difference.

The Liar

"It'll rain later," he said. "It said so on telly." It hadn't. "But tomorrow should be lovely, so the weatherperson said." Not that she had. And he said goodbye to them, as he needed to go to badminton.

But he wasn't going to badminton, as he didn't play, or watch, and didn't even like it. He went home. And spoke to his parents. They asked him about college, which he didn't go to any more (he had left months before, and he had spent that day in the pub). He then told them he needed money for books for his course, and once he had it, he went out with a girl who was not his girlfriend.

"I'm fed up of being single," he said. The young girl blushed at him. He told that he wanted to settle down, and that being faithful was the most important thing in a relationship. He said how his parents had divorced after one of them cheated, even though they had only ever had eyes for each other, and were currently on the sofa at his home watching telly. Then he sent a phone message to his girlfriend, telling the girl he was with that it was about going to a concert that didn't even exist.

He took the bus home. He struck up a conversation with a man about the local football team, and explained how a friend of his at the club said a new signing was on the brink of being unveiled. Nothing he had said that day had been true.

As he got off the bus, a magic fairy spied him. This magic fairy had particular skills. She could see into the future. In his future, he swindled people out of their savings, conned women on dating sites, and caused mayhem with a spider's web of lies. The magic fairy still didn't understand about why he lied about things that didn't matter.

But she had another power: she could ask a person a question, and they would tell the truth, even if they hardly knew it themselves. So she stepped in front of him (which must have been a bit of a shock, you don't get that many magic fairies at bus stops, as most have bicycles).

"You always tell lies, and the lies you tell are always wrong. Especially when they cause loss or upset to others. But why do you lie when there seems no point to it?"

The young man was about to spin a lie when the power of the magic fairy made him tell the truth. "I create a tapestry of lies. I lie to everyone, to get what I want, and to make others do as I wish. And if I ever told the truth, it might stand out differently in how I say it or act around saying it. And reveal everything else I say to be a lie. As lies are way of manipulating those around me, I cannot take that risk! Plus, I need to practice my lying, to hone it. So I speak lies even more convincingly than the truth!"

The magic fairy told him of his criminal future and of lives ruined at his hands. But she did so for herself, knowing he would carry on exactly the same.

Those who lie about trivial matters are likely to be engaged in a larger deception.

19

The Determined Woman and the Quest for Love

There was once a man of generally unremarkable qualities, but he caught the eye of a local woman. Finding he was single, she set upon making them a couple. She worked hard to make them closer, and would sometimes use opportunities to distance him from others. She would flatter his ego and try to wear things he would like. She asked him about himself, and made sure she asked many questions on subjects he knew he was interested in. He did not invite her attention, and would occasionally politely pour cold water upon it.

Time passed, and whilst they got on well enough, no romance had blossomed. She began to grow bitter at the efforts she had expended to no avail. Whereas before she would overstate his good points, she began to deride him behind his back. When he avoided her advances, her words became unkind.

They argued and she complained that for all her words and acts, they had not become a couple. The man looked her squarely in the eye. He told her that he had broken no promise to her. She had viewed him as prey, and he had responded accordingly. He was not her employer, and bound to promote her to girlfriend upon her saying and doing what she felt she should. They parted on angry terms and never spoke again.

If you treat someone as prey or prisoner, they will usually try to flee even pleasant surroundings.

20

The Drivers

He pootled along on the inside lane in his red car. No rush, he thought. A blue car whizzed past him. "Idiot racer," thought red car.

"Sunday driving moron," thought blue car.

A yellow car was in the outside lane had been behind the blue car. "He's a muppet for going too fast," he muttered, "and the one on the inside is just as bad for driving way too slowly."

A silver car was behind yellow car. "Why is this dweeb hogging the outside lane?" she said to herself.

The black car behind said to his passenger how the silver car was travelling far too closely to the yellow car. A mile later, the black car made a left turn.

The white car that also came off bemoaned that the black car hadn't indicated to come off. And beeped the black car.

"No need for that," chastised the orange car. And look at this fool in the van, trying to change lanes now. The orange car wondered whether they should let them in.

The van driver sweated, thinking how he had to get his passenger to the hospital to have their baby.

And the taxi driver looked at the traffic jam that was materialising, and lamented the driving standards on the road...as he blocked off the cyclist.

It is difficult to find peace and virtue in your own journey if you unduly obsess over the decisions of others.

The Unhappy Couple

A husband and wife were going through a period where they argued often. She went out to shop for a few items and saw a friend. Despite saying she would be home soon, she decided to go for a drink with her friend. They chatted, and a quick coffee led to going to a bar for gin. One led to another, and soon they had whiled away a good deal of the afternoon, and much of the evening. By the time the wife returned home, it had been many hours since she had said she was popping to the local shop. She knew her husband would not like her having been out, and did not wish to explain herself to him.

The husband had been wallpapering the house since before she left. He didn't like doing it, and he had grown grumpy at her not returning when she said she would. He resolved to tell her so when she came back. But the wife knew her husband well. When she came in, some seven hours after popping out, she immediately said, "I don't like the way you're doing that wallpaper." She then criticised various aspects of the wallpaper and his workmanship. He was so incensed that he forgot all about her strange disappearance, and focused all his efforts on defending his work. After a heated exchange, both went to bed not speaking to each other.

The angry can sometimes be easily fooled.

22

The Point

Two lawyers were given a case at very short notice, with each appearing for opposing sides. The paperwork for the case went to many thick folders full of documents.

The inexperienced lawyer tried to get a grasp of the whole thing, which was impossible in the time he had. By the time the case started, he was a nervous wreck and still understood little of the case.

The experienced lawyer had concentrated on what that specific hearing was about. He knew the point that was to be decided that day, and the limited part of the case he needed to know for that hearing. The court granted what he asked for, and he found the day straightforward.

When time is of the essence, concentrate on what you know you have to do first.

23

The Two Swordsmen

In ancient times, there was a great swordsman who was regarded as the finest of his day. Over many years, he had defeated many opponents. He had his own school, famous for its teaching.

A young swordsman went to visit the city where the school was at, dreaming of being able to enrol. However, through a small error he managed to insult a man he met shortly after arriving. That man was the great swordsman himself! The young swordsman apologised, but to no avail. The great swordsman told him that they were to fight at noon the next day.

Such fights were always to the death, and the young swordsman was gravely troubled. At best, he would kill a man he revered, all because of a minor disagreement. At worst, he would be killed. And the latter was far more likely. In fact, he considered it near a certainty. He decided to visit the man, and to speak to him.

However, their second meeting did not seem to go much better than the first. "Why should I back down? I do not care if it was an unintentional minor insult or not. You are scared. You are still learning your craft as a swordsman, whereas I have had nothing to learn for many years. I will see you tomorrow at noon!"

Initially, the young swordsman was crestfallen. However, he then analysed the man's words more carefully. The older man was clearly aggressive, to an irrational extent, and apparently had no capacity for mercy. His overconfidence and anger didn't seem to fit with him being a great swordsman. And then the young man thought about the comment that he had had nothing to learn for many years. That suggested a closed mind. As a talented swordsman himself, he now saw significant vulnerabilities to the legend he was meeting to duel with.

When noon came, the great swordsman seemed almost impatient. The young swordsman wondered how many men before him had been beaten by reputation alone. "Are you ready, young fool?"

"Before we begin, let me say this, to you and your students. I did not mean to offend you, and I have apologised. Yet despite your position of power, you offered no mercy. And yet you call yourself a teacher? You know nothing of my skills, yet you say I am the one to be scared. Overconfidence is not a mark of intelligence when it comes to combat. And you say you have had nothing to learn for years, which I interpret to mean you have given up on improving in any way, and so your ability has probably stagnated."

This enraged the great swordsman, and when they began to fight, he charged forwards maniacally. But the young swordsman was alert and well trained. And when the duel was over, it was the young man who walked away from it.

To stop learning is to give up slowly.

24

The Restructure

There was a large department of offices where they decided to restructure. This seemed to happen every few years, and there was an element of a merry-go-round about the way things were run.

Despite staff fatigue at management meddling, there was still much gossip about who might get some of the newly created posts, and who might leave.

There was one post of head manager advertised, as well as two deputy managers. Three existing managers seemed most likely to get those jobs. One was termed the "horrible manager". She was a nightmare to work with, for, under, or to herself manage. Another was called the "useless manager". This was with good cause, as he was useless. Every drama became a crisis, and no amount of hard work or help changed him. But somehow, he always got a managerial job. Finally, there was the "popular manager". He was respected, fair and well liked. He had worked hard to get where he was. Some people hoped he would become head manager, as he was clearly the best choice. Others knew that if he became head manager, they would have to be in the team of the "horrible" one or the "useless" one. And for that reason only, they liked the idea of him getting a position as deputy manager (as long as he was their line manager).

On the morning of the appointments, both the horrible manager and the useless manager seemed rather cheery. But when they say the popular manager, he was by far the happiest. The staff then received an email. The deputy managers' jobs would go to the horrible one and the useless one. But the head manager's job was an external candidate. They were stunned, and one approached the popular manager.

"I'm so sorry, you were robbed!"

"Oh no, I'm very happy!"

"How can you be happy?"

"Well… I thought about the jobs. Would you want to manage either of the new deputy managers? They are nightmares! I'm not sure I could do it. And the staff would think I could fix things, when I am not sure that is possible in the current situation. And what about if I got a deputy manager post? All the time clashing with the horrible one or useless one, with the other one in charge? So I thought about demotion. But then I'd still be working for one of them! Probably worse! I'm not sure I would have managed any option, even for the money they offered. So I applied for a job elsewhere. And I got it! It looks like it will really suit me, and I could do with a change. It's a good job, I'm very happy. I know what the other managers are like, and I know what I'm like, and this is the best option for me. Thank you for your kind words though."

Knowing others is wisdom, knowing yourself is enlightenment.

24

Laughter Girl

There was once a television programme with lots of people on it. It was an unexpected hit. Various members of the cast were acclaimed. One stood out. "I love her laugh," people would say. "We want more of her on telly!" the cries came.

And she began to be interviewed on chat shows and the like. "Now people love your laugh, don't they?" And she would laugh. And the interviewer would laugh. And the audience would laugh. And everyone would say, "She should have her own show, she only needs to laugh. We love her!" And her popularity went across the board. She won an award for best television newcomer.

So the producers gave her a show of her own. They made sure there were plenty of opportunities for her to laugh. There was even an advert playing during the commercial break which she was on. Predictably, she was laughing in it.

By the third episode of the new show, many people had turned off. "All she does is laugh." "I'm sick of that laugh."

A year later, she tried to relaunch her career. Firstly, she tried it without the laugh. "Oh, she used to be so happy. She's a miserable so and so now!" Then she added the laugh back in. "I preferred it when she was miserable, she's giving me a headache." Then she tried some new things, and the critics said she was pretty good. But she didn't get far, because the audience had decided they didn't want to know by then.

Overkill can make the trendiest uncool.

25

The Big Presentation

An office was having their head manager attending to give them a talk. She was unpopular, and she was also lacking in charm, understanding of the issues and figures and pretty much any redeeming qualities that the staff could think of. She had much in common with their local manager.

He warned the staff against any snide remarks. His track record as a manager showed that he was adept at bullying and getting away with it. And so the staff faced a day of hellish boredom that stopped them doing their jobs, and knew that they could say little against it without formal or informal penalty. It had all happened before.

So when the day of the meeting came, both the head manager and local manager thought it would go smoothly. This only seemed to be reinforced when the staff were in their seats waiting for the talk to begin. And when there were polite and serious questions about the issues, the managers thought they had the staff in the palm of their hands.

But the questions kept coming. And they were well-researched questions. When the managers replied that these were serious issues, the staff said that indeed they were. Perhaps they should have further training? Focus groups? Some had prepared some documents they thought should be considered. And whilst the managers had thought they wouldn't take the issue seriously, they were united in their steadfastly austere consideration of the issues. It got to a stage where the head manager asked if they were "being funny" by how seriously they were considering things. The staff expressed displeasure and concern that they didn't care about these important issues, and questioned his commitment to them. And the look of the head manager at him showed the first signs of a split.

By the end of the first coffee break, the managers were exhausted. By the end of the second, the staff were bubbling with references to "minutes, focus groups, further training, guidance on the protocol, training on the policy, and synergized progression".

As the day drew to an end, it was the managers who were watching the clock. "Can you shortlist people to head up a group on all this, touch base and then cascade it down? Maybe get a checklist ready for a global arrival by the next meeting? And maybe we could pencil the date for that in now?"

The head manager looked downright angry. Throughout the day she had told them that she felt they were mocking her. But they had replied with denial, then polite outrage, and then a concerned, "This is beginning to sound like bullying..." At which point someone happened to have the work policies to hand, as well as some government guides.

"I'm not pencilling in anything!" And she walked off. And the next "meeting" was actually an email (though the managers still called it a meeting), and the staff smiled and smiled.

The best way to mock pomposity is sometimes to treat it with utter seriousness.

26

The Perfect Couple

Andrew and Kelly had been together about three years when he proposed. They were besides themselves with excitement for their wedding.

It hadn't been plain sailing. Andrew was living his life down the rugby club, for one thing. And that beard had to go. Whereas Andrew wouldn't have Kelly's dogs sleeping on the bed. And her sister was a cow. "I know she's your sister, but grow a backbone and stand up to that evil witch!" However, the rugby and chess playing mortgage advisor, and the baking-mad optician who had four pets and a horse decided they had so much in common it was "almost scary"!

Kelly dieted hard for the wedding. She went down three dress sizes! Whereas Andrew learnt to dance (his refusal to dance when they were out had been a source of friction before).

And their family and friends clapped, cried and drank like fish on the happy day. Andrew stood up, in fake tan because Kelly didn't want him looking too pale next to her. "From day one, I knew I'd marry this girl. She's perfect, and I wouldn't change a thing about her!"

Kelly shed a tear, the emotion a welcome break from thinking her dress would cut her in half. "And I wouldn't change a thing about my husband either! From day one, he's been perfect! Perfect!"

And the happy couple kissed. And he wondered if Kelly would do the things that Kevin and Jessica did, as she took heed of her mother's advice on how to take control of him.

Partners may say they wouldn't change a thing about the other whilst setting about a list of alterations.

27

The Right Circumstances

She used to exercise a way back. We're not talking about back in school. After that. It was quite fun, a social thing too. But then it seemed to fade out. Getting to places seemed about the speed, rather than the journey. The emphasis was on where they'd park, and planning their route. Once upon a time, they'd walk for hours and never get there, and that was just fine.

She had to get fit. She wasn't totally unfit, but it had been on her mind for a while. She wasn't doing the New Year's Resolution thing though. The gyms were full of new starters who were gone in a month. And the pavements were too hard for running. Plus, how many joggers look healthy?

The dark nights didn't help. She got an exercise video. But she could have used more room to do it in the lounge, really. Maybe she'd clear out the spare room? That thought stayed as an idea though.

Then she had it. She'd join an exercise class. The first one was a shock to the system. And the second. She rested the third. Then her arm felt a bit achy, so she left it. But she'd be back the week after. A month later, she felt a bit awkward going after having missed so much.

So walking it was. But it was the same old route, pretty quickly. She needed someone to make her.

Which was when she joined the gym, and got a personal trainer. And she was great! And she couldn't say why she lapsed, but she did. Maybe she needed a different programme?

Then there was a block of work and social engagements, and exercise fell into the background. And then she had cold after cold. But she got well in time for Christmas, and another round of parties and things to do.

She really had to get fit next year. But not the gym, when it was busy with all the new starters...

If you wait for circumstances to be perfect, you may be wasting a time when circumstances are good enough.

28

Have You Ever Met an Unhappy Bee?

There was a woman who had a job. And she loved her job. But then she met a man, and she loved him much more. And they had children, who she loved more again. And life was pretty wonderful.

But in time, her husband passed. Her children helped her through the initial stages of grief, but they lived far away. And when she overcame grief, it seemed only emptiness was there to replace it. And the days were a struggle, and she did not seem able to rise from the rut.

Eventually she took his clothes to a local charity shop. Somehow she found herself agreeing to help out. She didn't plan to; she wanted to be on her own. She'd tell them she wouldn't turn up. Or she'd just not go.

But she went.

Suddenly she was being trained. At her time of life?

There was a charity run. She was asked if she would help. She heard herself agreeing. It was actually quite a long, hard day. Strangely, she liked that. She'd be helping with things like that again.

Her children expressed concern that she might be overdoing it. But when they saw her, she looked better. Healthier. Happier.

The charity shop said they needed another acting manager. She wondered who it would be. After some cajoling and her first job application in 30 years, it turned out to be her.

One rainy Wednesday afternoon, she was arranging much welcomed refreshments for the staff when a woman came in. She had her late husband's clothes. Her eyes were a little red.

She smiled at the woman. "We're having a cup of tea, and you must have one too."

Industry can help overcome misery.

29

The Prey

The boys weren't just friends: they were a gang. And as with most gangs, the admittance fee was a lowering of morality and a dangerously evolving arrogance. Power like that seeks out weakness. And so it was that the smallest boy in their school became a target for their stares and taunts.

When he stopped looking at them, they had to make him. To see his panic in his eyes thrilled them. And so they would surround him and push him, before letting him run off.

Their concerns were teachers who were switched on (that varied a lot), and busybody pupils who thought what they were doing was wrong. It was no big deal. In their view.

It was getting boring, anyway. They hardly had to do anything and he'd run off or cry or both. They decided to stop. But they'd have a finale first.

After some planning, they had people watching for teachers and witnesses from three directions. Then they'd box him in from all sides, and torment him. This time he'd have nowhere to run. There was a tacit understanding they'd rough him up, but this was more about intimidation rather than actual violence. There was just no need with him.

Everything was going like clockwork, and they descended upon him that lunchtime. With all their sentries, there were three to carry it out.

He caught sight of them out of the corner of his eye, and he turned to go to the left. Blocked. Then the right. But that was blocked too. They grinned as he visibly shook. Time seemed to go slow as they got closer and closer. He edged into the wall, and they looked down on him as he cowered pathetically.

They looked at each other and laughed. And that was when the first one felt the rock against his jaw. He went down and didn't get up. He kicked the second one so hard between the legs that he stayed in hospital overnight. The last one couldn't say the element of surprise overcame him, but he was on his own, and that foxed him. The small boy punched him in the face and ran off. And every day that followed, the erstwhile gang were reminded of what they brought upon themselves that day.

A cornered mouse will bite even a cat.

It's Cold Outside

There were once two sisters. They were both pretty nice, studied hard, and worked hard. They got on well, and in many ways they were similar. But they were most certainly different in one respect.

The younger sister careful (her sister said too careful). "Everyone's got colds this time of year, I'm not going there." "The beach? At this time of year? We'll freeze!" "I am not hanging about watching your boyfriend play football when I'll be eating an hour later than usual, and it will probably rain!"

Her older sister had always been the one to grab a jacket and head for the door... and then wait for her sister to put on her scarf, hat, gloves, and do every button up (although she always seemed to do all her buttons up, she never seemed to get fast at doing it).

As the years went on, each became more pronounced in their ways. The older sister entered muddy obstacle courses, and the younger sister eschewed anything with risks of rain, cold, or people with colds. Each annoyed the other. The older sister wanted her sister with her, and the younger one was frustrated how she still got more colds than her sibling.

Over one of their marathon tea-drinking sessions, the younger sister asked (again) how her sister somehow managed to generally be healthier than her?

"Well, I've conditioned myself, haven't I? My system as well. I don't shield myself totally from all the day-to-day risks, a bit of cold or a drop of rain. So I get used to it.

Although I have taken note of you a bit; I don't want to be sat there freezing or soaking through. Plus, apparently if you do something good, it boosts your immune system. Your body too, if it involves fitness."

The younger sister pondered this. "You may have a point... Yes, I really said that. Okay, sign me up for an obstacle course. But I'm first in the shower when we get home!"

Beware the protection isn't worse than the risk.

32

The Marathon in an Invisible Maze

One day, an alien was looking at Earth. She was a bit bored, and decided to entertain herself. She could be a bit terrifying, although she was also very wise and had magnificent ears. She decided to kidnap three humans.

"Humans," she said, "I will not harm you. You have been brought here to test yourselves and to learn. You shall be returned to Earth soon." Sooner if you're really annoying, she thought.

The alien had selected people of some mental firmness, and so they were able to cope with what was happening. She further explained, "You will each have to race. This will be in a maze. You will not see it as I shall have your eyes shielded. Also, the maze is invisible."

"How shall we know where we are going? Won't it be dangerous?"

"How far is it? How do we know the way if we can't see?" asked another.

"They look faster than me, that can't be fair!" protested the third.

The alien smiled with both mouths. "It is fair, as you will be running against yourself. The way is as far as it is, and the obstacles are largely up to you. Your mind will set your direction on the true path, and you should take careful note of that. This is not a normal race."

"Aliens!" the three humans thought. "Never a straight answer!"

It was not long after that they set forth on their challenge.

The first resolved to get on with it. They weren't overly confident, but equally at least they knew they were trying and apparently getting somewhere.

The second decided they must be doing well. They had always thought they were a bit fitter than they were, and they'd be able to coast because they were so good.

The third dreaded it. The problem wasn't the nature of the race, although that didn't help. It was them. They weren't good at this sort of thing. It wasn't that they couldn't run, it was that the circumstances weren't helping. And they weren't happy with their speed. It felt wrong, and they were doing it wrong. They could do better than this! But they weren't, and it was only their fault.

A time later, the first runner suddenly arrived at the finish line. "Well done," said the alien. "Your mind was balanced so your progress was strong."

It was a long time afterwards that the second came in. "Did I win?" they said, as they were able to see again.

"No," said the alien. "You were second. You would have been second even if you went the same distance as the first runner, but you didn't. Your hubris took you off the true path, and so you ended up going a very long way around."

A protracted time passed before the third person finished. "I knew I'd be last, I could tell. I'm not very good and…"

The alien cut them off. "You had just as much chance of finishing first as any, I assure you. You spent precious time and energy on being hard on yourself. You did not stray from the path as much as the human who finished second, but your constant self-criticism held you back. It was that which added to and exacerbated your fatigue. To the winner, I would suggest you guard against complacency. For those of you who finished second and third, do not be your own worst enemy, by false praise or habitual negativity."

Over confidence will lead you away from the true path. Whereas being overcritical of yourself will set you back and tire you out. Seek a happy balance.

33

Regally Blonde

There once was a girl who wanted to grow up to be a lawyer. She worked hard. Often she would speak to people of her dream, and of her hair, which was a golden blonde. And she would have compliments on both, and on her determination in one so young. It was her focus, especially when she was studying, had exams, or was awaiting results. Which was most of the time. It was all she really spoke of with any regularity, apart from her hair.

During her twenties, she became a fully qualified lawyer. It was no surprise to friends and family how her excitement led her to speak tirelessly of her accomplishment and future, as well as her golden locks. But this did not change with time. She did not just consider herself the most important person in the room, but the only important person in the room.

Years went by, and many young men were attracted to her. She would swish her blonde hair and ask them what it was like to be with such a successful, stunning blonde. Most of them would get bored of her only interests being her, her work and her hair. Indeed, one boyfriend (upon their parting) said that she should consider changing, and that he didn't think much of her job or her hair. She thought him ill-mannered and unsuitable for her. She sought a gentleman to appreciate her, and to treat her as his princess.

And then she found a man who seemed entranced by her talking about how clever she had been, and how beautiful she looked, and agreeing with her when she inferred he should do so. They married, and happy years followed. But there came a day when the man, who was actually a much more interesting and lovely individual than she, became bored of her endless self-aggrandizement. And the pair divorced. And when she finally met somebody new, she talked of herself rarely and without much joy.

Those who are self-obsessed leave little room left for love and friendship to take hold.

The Three Monks

Three monks were working the gardens in front of the monastery when they saw a man arguing on the phone. He was clearly incensed and struggling to control his vitriol.

"How awful it must be to be so angry!" one said.

"And how out of control," said another.

The third monk thought a moment and said, "Worst still, to feel and act like that about a fellow human being." They agreed that this was the wisest comment of them all.

Unfortunately for them, the man on the phone had heard every word. He strode over to them and looked agitatedly at them. "What do you know? In your false environment? You know nothing!" And he went to turn away.

But the monks were set to protest the skills they had been taught. "We at least know tolerance!" "And patience!" added another. "And the love of our fellow man," they cooed.

The man turned back. "Is that so? I bet you would be far worse than me in comparable circumstances. And I'd wager on that fact!"

"We are not rich men and we have nothing to wager with. Otherwise we would be only too pleased to demonstrate the truth of our words."

But the man said they could bet their gardening against him making a contribution to the monastery, and they agreed. They set upon rules that he could do nothing truly bad, painful or inappropriate to them, and they would be honest in how they felt.

"Oh I'll do better than that," said the man. "I will give you things that are much sought after, where you need not do much, and which do not conflict with your faith."

The monks thought how the abbot would be pleased with them demonstrating their faith, getting money for the monastery, and helping the man realise he should be kinder in his thoughts to his fellow man.

Several months passed as each monk underwent a separate trial. At the end of it, all three found themselves tending to the man's garden.

"He somehow arranged for me to share an inheritance with a friend! Well, I say friend, but I will never speak to that man again! And I do not even care for worldly possessions! I cannot deny being angry beyond belief!"

"I went on holiday. It should have been glorious. The weather was. But the people I went with! And I was allowed to pick them! I do not plan to venture far from the monastery again unless the abbot makes me do so. It was terrible. Terrible!"

"That's nothing," replied the third, "I had to stay in a lovely house. But the neighbours? The neighbours?! Better solitary confinement in a prison!"

Do not assume love of your fellow man until you have shared an inheritance, been on holiday with them, or lived next to them.

The Woman Who Sent Lots of Messages

There was a woman who liked a man. She obtained his phone number, and expressed her interest. His reply was friendly, but distinctly lukewarm concerning romance. Undeterred, she repeatedly phoned and messaged the man. Sometimes she would get a reply, and sometimes she would not. On some subjects, he did answer fully. Some might have said he was trying to let her down gently, or to offset turning her down by being helpful or friendly. As far as she was concerned, she was making headway in her romantic ambitions, albeit slowly.

She would deliberately message in vague terms. She spoke of a large event that was happening locally, and that they may see each other there. He agreed that they might. Sometimes he had little time to answer her. Given that she was not taking the obvious hint that he was not interested, he was placed in a difficult situation. His short answers or not answering her at all had not stopped her messages, and he felt he had conveyed that he wasn't interested in her that way, or any way.

It didn't work. At the next large local event, she messaged to ask if "they" were going. He said he didn't know if she was, and he had not made a decision himself. She replied flippantly that he was playing hard to get. She said they should go together. He said he didn't think that was a good idea, and that she should find a man right for her and go with him.

The hint did not take hold. She made several more attempts to get him to meet her, which was met with a mix of silence, evasion and friendly chit-chat. But never a yes, and a repeated message between the lines of no.

She grew frustrated waiting for the man, and they argued. "You blow hot and cold," she said, "and you don't know what you want!"

"But I have never agreed to go out with you, or suggested I did, or suggested I liked you that way."

"Sometimes you are all chatty, and you know I like you. The you'll go quiet, but you'll always start speaking again." The man thought of saying he was only replying after she repeatedly messaged, but he realised his words were falling on deaf ears.

The woman went off in a huff, leaving the man bemused.

If you look for small changes in people to justify your argument or belief, you'll probably find them. But that doesn't mean your conclusions are convincing or correct.

36

The Woman Who Drove Forward

There was once a married couple. They didn't have things too easy, but neither did they have things that hard. He would go to work, and she would take care of everything else. They were contented, but sometimes they struggled a bit with their finances. He would hold her close, and say things would be alright. And she felt good in his arms, and things were alright.

But she wanted them to be more than alright for both of them. And she studied and learnt to drive. And a part-time job to save for a car led to her having a car, a qualification and a job she could do whilst still looking after the home. And she was very pleased with the sum of her efforts. She put her arms around him, and said things would definitely be alright. She thought they would be happier than ever.

She was wrong. Just as things appeared to be as ideal as she could get them, he left her. She was inconsolable for a time, particularly as he left her for another woman. She thought this woman must be better than her. Prettier, younger, slimmer. Her imagination tormented her with images of them at trendy parties and suchlike, even though she knew she was being daft.

But the self-belief that had got her to pass the exams she had, to learn to drive, and to get the job, was still in her (albeit a bit bruised). And she found another man, a very nice man. And the two came to discuss their former partners. "And I obviously wasn't good enough for him, just at the time everything else seemed to be going right."

Her new man chuckled, which she would have thought harsh had she not known his character. "You think it is a coincidence that he ended the relationship just after you qualified, got the job, passed your driving test and got your car?" She looked at him quizzically. "For years he had been the big man, the powerhouse, not that there is necessarily anything wrong in that. But you had found your own power, and good for you. But it affected him, and he couldn't take it."

She looked uncertain at his answer, so he carried on. "What else had changed in your relationship?"

"Nothing."

"And it was fine before?"

"Definitely, it changed almost overnight."

And whilst she had previously imagined so many ways in which she was not deemed good enough for her ex, it suddenly made sense that her success was something he could not take.

Your good points can drive someone away as easily as the "bad" sometimes.

37

The Four Siblings

There was a friendly family rivalry between two brothers and two sisters. As they were all into fitness, they decided to enter a local obstacle course.

The first trained, but knew it would be very hard. Probably too hard. He had seen people who had failed, people who he estimated fitter than him. As the day of the race approached, his nerves got the better of him. By race day, he was a mess, and he did not finish the race.

The second did not understand what there was to be worried about. She trained, she felt ready. But when she arrived and saw the course, her heart sank. This seemed too tough. And the athletes around her were a different level. Whilst she was getting around the course, she felt she was never going to complete such a scary-looking race, and so pulled out after she felt she had done enough.

The third had a plan of training, but didn't do most of it. He didn't research the course at all, and probably wasn't fit enough to do it (despite initially thinking he could). As the miles wore on, the thought of carrying on was too much for him, and he pulled out.

The wisest of the four was the other sister. She did not discount what was said about the course, and realised it looked an ominous task. But she saw how it could be done, and had trained hard with this in mind. She was the only one of them to complete the course.

Fear of a thing (or person), often comes from its reputation, its appearance, or inadequate preparation to face it. You must conquer all to maximise your chances of success.

38

The Sword

A martial artist was struggling to reach the next level. He knew a significant number of techniques for sparring, and he would try this and that without making much progress.

His asked his teacher, a Japanese woman, for advice. "Learn from the sword," she said and smiled.

Her English was not perfect (although much better than his Japanese), and he reasoned that she must be telling him to learn about the sword. He respected her understanding greatly, and soon he knew the parts of the sword, as well as its history. He didn't really get how this would help, but he imagined it might be that he'd learn something without realising, or that his study would distract him from his problems.

His sparring did not improve. He asked a friend, and they said maybe the teacher meant that he should learn swordsmanship. Firstly, he researched about masters of the art. Then he practiced with a wooden sword. Strangely (in his mind), his throwing skills improved, but not his sparring. Fearful of appearing to challenge the teacher's words, he resolved to ask a senior grade what he should do.

The senior grade chuckled. "I believe I understand. And the teacher said exactly what she intended to say. When you spar, you are a bit half-hearted. I do not mean you are feinting, which is different; you are indecisive. You clearly have skill and ideas, but your level of confidence and experience means that you don't do that much with them. And sooner or later, you are picked off. You need to commit to what you are doing. The sword acts or doesn't act. There is no half-measure."

The student considered this and said, "But what if what I commit to is the wrong choice? Especially when I am making my decisions in a heartbeat."

The senior grade nodded his head. "That is a real possibility. But sometimes you need 100% commitment to acting or not acting, or you cannot even hope to win."

Sometimes you need the way of the sword. Make your decision and commit to it fully.

The Tough Guys

There were once two brothers who drew the ire of a local gang. Although they had done nothing wrong, the gang plotted to fight them both. The brothers were known to be skilled in martial arts, and boxed, and the gang decided to tackle them separately.

One half of the gang tracked one brother until they found him alone. They shouted abuse and threats, and advanced on him. The gang had made him angry, but he would not let that affect him being an effective fighter. He was strong and fast, and struck the first man who came towards him hard. When the second man approached, he took him down. A few minutes later, he had somehow managed to defeat the men, who now laid on the floor injured or unconscious.

The other half of the gang tried a similar plan with the second brother. Again, they shouted all manner of insults. They said how they would beat him up. The brother did nothing. They goaded him, but he did not respond. They were menacing, but he did not turn a hair. He expected them to come forward and attack him at any moment...but they did not. Part of him wanted to hurt them, but he controlled it. Firstly, because he knew they wanted him to lose his cool and dive in, to be surrounded by them. Secondly, their words hadn't really been backed up with much at that stage. After a stand-off, the gang seemed to lose confidence or interest, and left. Disbelievingly, the brother found the safest route home, wondering quite how the events had turned.

Upon meeting at home, the two brothers talked of their crazy day. The one who had gotten away without fighting said his brother had achieved the impossible by besting so many opponents. His brother was glad to be uninjured after such a brawl, but said his brother's icy cool was something very special. When he heard of the extreme way the gang had repeatedly goaded his brother to fight, he marvelled at his brother, the "ice man".

Lao-Tzu: "He who conquers others is strong, he who conquers himself is mighty."

40

The Lovely Boy

There was once a couple who were blessed with eight children. They were good parents, and whilst they had no favourites, both they and seven of the children treated the baby with special care. Although the parents were always busy, the baby had to come first. And as he grew up, it became the nature of things for both parents and siblings to dote on the youngest. All of them spoke of his gifts with pride.

He was bright, and with strong support he did very well at school. There was always someone with time for him, and they enjoyed helping him. His hard work paid off (as did that of the family collective), and he went to university. He succeeded with his studies, again with a range of help from his family.

And so this pattern progressed into his professional life. He had become used to brothers and sisters ironing his shirts, or giving him lifts, or whatever assistance it was every few days. Because the help was shared between many, the others had taken longer to tire of it. And it had become expected by him by now. The family were happy at his achievements, and still engaged in nostalgia of the baby that he was. But he was no longer the youngest, for some of his brothers and sisters now had children themselves.

One woman hooked him as her husband. She did everything for him, consciously or unconsciously having picked up a theme in how he lived his life. And thinking that he must be worth it, for his family treated him that way.

In work, he had progressed to a point where he could make demands on junior staff, sometimes unfairly. And he did so. But they did not speak of him kindly, as his family did.

And some of the children of his brothers and sisters were of an age where they would have benefitted from his guidance, for they hoped to follow the path he had taken for university and career. But he ignored their requests, because he did not wish to help. He was surprised when their parents said he was ungrateful, and had done little for others when he had been helped so much. He said how they always said he was their lovely baby brother, but they said that was a long time ago; they did not like the man he had grown into.

His wife tired of doing everything for him. Since his family didn't do much for him now (some did not even speak to him), why should she? And he handled the situation with the skill of a man used to taking far more than giving. It was not long before they were being divorced.

But he was still the successful one... Except there were cutbacks. And he was unpopular with other staff, particularly junior members of staff. And he found himself at a new firm, and with a new life. And nobody ever said how he was such a beautiful baby boy, because that was a different time, a long, long time ago.

Debts not repaid will usually lead to penalties.

41

The Students

A group of friends decided to take up Tae Kwon Do.

The first said he was the strongest, so he would be the best. The second said they were faster, so they would be better. In turn, each listed the qualities they felt would make the most difference, linking them with themselves or another and pointing to their future success. Members of the group mentioned flexibility, stamina, memory, and who was the sportiest. Some months into their training, several of them had given up. Within a few years, only two were training.

Years later, there was only one left, and he came to pass his black belt grading.

The teacher and student recalled when he was just one of a group of friends starting training, and the student told him of the conversation they had concerning their respective strengths. "Which one do you think I was?" he asked the teacher.

The teacher didn't even need to think about it. "The most determined," he said.

Determination often outstrips ability.

42

The Javelin

There were two young javelin throwers making their debut in the same adult competition. Both had fathers who had competed. Ahmed's father had been a real talent, but Jamal's father was a legend in the sport, nationally and internationally.

It was fair to say that this fact only served to make Ahmed more anxious. How much special knowledge had Jamal's father imparted to him? How many unique opportunities to hone his craft and compete at the highest level had Jamal had? Ahmed theorized that when his father, wonderful as he was, got him tea whilst he threw in the rain, Jamal's father was probably taking Jamal to see a host of current champions for secret tips!

Why, even at the competition, Jamal would be getting told how to psyche Ahmed out (as well as the rest of the field), and make the most of the conditions on the day. It wasn't even close to fair!

Fortunately, Ahmed's father kept him as calm and as ready as he could. When they arrived at the stadium, he didn't see Jamal or his father. It was only just before they were set to compete that he saw Jamal. Somebody was telling him how his father was a legend, and they also loved him for his television work and the acting he'd more recently done.

Ahmed's father told him to get on with warming up, that this was about his throwing, nobody else's. And slowly, Ahmed began to focus more. Soon, the competition was afoot.

Ahmed was throwing well, and his father was keeping him upbeat and refreshed. With his last throw, he moved into bronze medal position.

Jamal placed tenth. The young men spoke afterwards and it was the start of a lifelong friendship.

"Your dad, he's just a legend, I mean some of the throws I've seen him do. At the Olympics, that just blew my mind!"

Jamal laughed. "Yeah, great throw. I think it is so cool that your dad comes though. Mine hardly ever makes it, he's always doing some media thing. He hasn't seen me compete in two years. I mean, we get on, but not like you and your dad. Must be good having him there?"

"Yeah," said Ahmed. And suddenly he viewed his own father as the real legend as far as he was concerned.

A great man does not always make a great father.

43

Tricks of the Trade

The judge turned to the prosecutor for her opening speech. She got through it, but her nerves and inexperience showed. The older defence advocate put forward his opening speech with more assuredness and eloquence.

After several witnesses, the court adjourned for lunch. The two lawyers found themselves wandering to the nearby shops for something to eat, and they fell into conversation.

"I was so nervous this morning! I know the case inside out, and I'd written down loads of notes, but it just feels so weird and new!" said the prosecutor.

"Ah, you'll get into it. I only started last year. I was nervous too!"

"What, you've only been doing it a year?"

"Mature student. I was a nurse before!"

The prosecutor was amazed. "But you were so confident, so calm! How do you do it?"

"Well I didn't start very confidently or good. Almost nobody does. But I got told how to make life easy for myself. You know you have notes of exactly what you want to say?" She nodded. "Well if you just read them, you'll lose eye contact, your words won't flow, and you'll lack impact."

"I realised that," she said, "I tried to leave my notes a bit, but then I got lost. A friend tried bullet points, but they struggled to string a sentence together at the start."

The defence advocate smiled. "Well I got a tip, and it works for me. I type exactly what I'm going to say for a few paragraphs. So I don't have to think so much, and I get more comfortable addressing the court. Then I do bullet points. By now my words are flowing, and I can engage more with the judge or magistrates. Look them in the eye, articulate with a bit more feeling. It has helped me, anyway."

"I wish you'd told me this morning, I might have won then!"

He smiled. "Oh I wouldn't have any concerns about that, my client has a skill at convicting himself!"

Learning the tricks of the trade can make your life much easier.

44

The Troubles of Timmywiggle

Timothy looked back at his mother. He was 4, and today was his first day at school. "I don't want to go," he had cried. But she had held his hand and kissed his brow. And she had bid him farewell.

The next day was worse. "I have to go back? But the teachers are monsters? And the other children are strange! Apart from one girl… but I hate it there, I hate it!"

His mother held back a tear as she led him in. "It'll be alright, Timmywiggle!" But she didn't feel so confident inside. Maybe she'd need to move schools or home school him. And whilst she struggled with the situation, Timmywiggle was far, far more emotional.

But by the next day, he was fine. Two weeks later, he admitted liking part of school. And it didn't take long before he was bored.

A slightly less emotional repeat of this occurred when he went to secondary school. The same pattern followed.

When his mother went to leave him at university, both were nervous. But by now, they were sensing a pattern of episodic crises. A cycle of nerves, her still calling him "Timmywiggle" (despite serious warnings to please stop), a period of agitation or mild hysteria, and the situation becoming rather more humdrum. Like his first day as a doctor, his first operation, his first day as a consultant, and even his first day as Prime Minister.

Time often reduces today's drama to tomorrow's drudgery.

45

The Global Ombudsman

There was a man who was not very happy. He'd studied for exams, and he had not done as well as he wanted. That got him thinking on the way his training hadn't got him the level of fitness he thought he would. And he had friends who were richer. He decided to write a complaint to the Global Ombudsman. Rather surprisingly, he had a reply, which invited him into the offices.

The man was led to the waiting room. He sat next to a dog, who was reading the paper. "Hiya mate, what are you in here for?" So the man began to list his complaints.

The dog waved him away, "Nothing, mate. I'm here for the sense of smell. Mine is about 1% to 10% of that of a bloodhound's. Flipping insulting, that is!" The man tried to explain that the dog actually had a powerful sense of smell, but the dog wasn't having it.

"That dog is obsessed with smell! All he ever talks about." The man realised the voice was coming from a penguin who was half inside a fish tank. "Do you know how much krill a blue whale can have a day? Four tonnes! How is that fair? I like krill, and that would keep me going for... has anyone got a calculator?" But they didn't, and the room grew quiet.

"Krill!" came a voice from the window. The bird on it mocked. "Do you know how far I can fly without a break? And the albatross manages 10,000 miles! Imagine poor me, just flying for tens of miles and feeling the pace?"

At that point, he was called through to speak with an advisor.

"Umm, about these exams...we actually have it that you were very lucky in the set of exams before."

"Yes, that's correct. I didn't really work hard enough for those, but I got lucky on the questions."

"And this time you got less lucky."

"Yes."

"So are you complaining about your luck, but only when it is bad luck?"

"That's quite right, yes."

The advisor fiddled with his glasses. "Umm...maybe we'll skip to the complaint about others being richer? I take it there is no complaint regarding those you're better off than?"

"Oh no, quite happy with that."

"So you've mentioned someone here, and note you feel you should be richer than them. Do you just want to be them?"

"No! No, sorry. Same money, just younger. And I don't like his wife, so not married to her. Or his job. Awful job. But the money, I'll have that." The advisor huffed and puffed and his red pen scribbled. "You're going to dismiss my complaint, aren't you?"

"Oh we don't dismiss complaints. Or uphold them. No need. You don't get anything for complaining to us, only when you ask us. And yes, it is different."

The man was disappointed. "Oh well, I guess at least you would have agreed with me, if it was allowed."

The advisor thoughtfully bit his lip for a moment. Then he said, "No. We all have the occasional moan, but to complain when you're blessed like you are either means you're a fool or ungrateful."

And the man left, and when he came to realise his error, resolved to be less of a fool.

Have perspective on your complaints of life, or others will complain of your lack of perspective.

Printed in Great Britain
by Amazon